P9-DHS-303

Especially for my Mum and Dad

Viking
Published by the Penguin Group
Penguin Books USA Inc., 375 Hudson Street, New York, New York 10014, U.S.A
Penguin Books Australia Ltd, Ringwood, Victoria, Australia
Penguin Books Canada Ltd, 10 Alcorn Avenue, Toronto, Ontario, Canada M4V 3B2
Penguin Books (N.Z.) Ltd, 182–190 Wairau Road, Auckland 10, New Zealand

First published in Great Britain by All Books for Children,
a division of the All Children's Company Ltd., 1993
First American edition published by Viking,
a division of Penguin Books USA Inc., 1994

1 3 5 7 9 10 8 6 4 2

Library of Congress Catalog Card Number: 93-60709
ISBN 0-670-85353-6
Printed in Singapore

Winter Rabbit

Patrick Yee

Viking

"It's snowing, Bear!"
"It's snowing, Squirrel!"

"Shall we build
a friend, Squirrel?"

"Okay, Bear.
First the body."

"And here's his head."

"Look, Squirrel,
he's a rabbit."
"A winter rabbit."

"Two round stones for his eyes, and a great big smile."

"Look, Bear,
he's finished."

“We have a friend!”

"Has he come to play with us…

…before our winter sleep, Bear?"

"Yes!"

"Hello, Rabbit!"

"Bear and I need to
eat before our
winter sleep,
Rabbit."

"Squirrel needs nuts
and I like fish. Here's
a carrot for you, Rabbit."

"But it's too hard for him to eat, Bear."

"Then I'll make a
snow carrot for him."

"Look, Bear, he loves it!"

"Let's take him to the ice pond, Bear."
"Do you think he can skate, Squirrel?"

“Try to stand up.”

“He can do it!”

“Oh, Squirrel, look at him!”

"Hurray!"

"Look, Squirrel, someone else has been here!"

"And they're throwing snowballs."

"Let's get them!"

"Ready! Aim!"

"Fire!"

"It's our friends, the Polar Bears."

"What can you do in the snow, Rabbit?"

"What's he doing?"

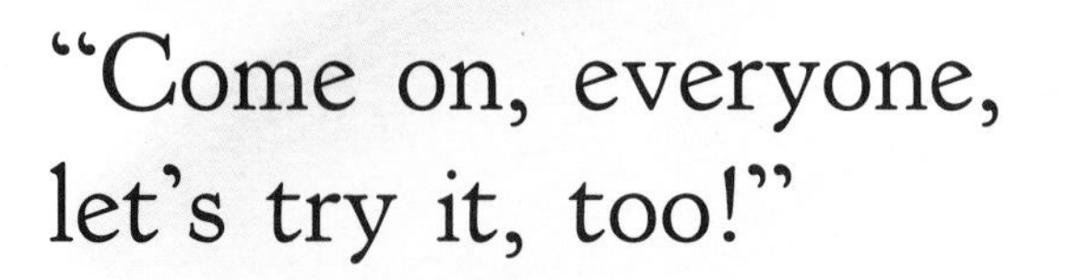

“Come on, everyone,
let’s try it, too!”

"Snow angels!"

"Time for a
last ride, Rabbit." WHOOSH!

"Good-bye,
Polar Bears!"
"What a wonderful
day, Rabbit."

“We’re tired now, Rabbit.
It’s time for our long
winter sleep.”

"Sleep tight, Bear."
"Sweet dreams, Squirrel."

"Good-bye, Rabbit.
See you next winter."